CREEP OUT

TOMBS

VALERIE BODDEN

CREATIVE EDUCATION

Published by Creative Education
P.O. Box 227, Mankato, Minnesota 56002
Creative Education is an imprint of The Creative Company
www.thecreativecompany.us

Design and production by Chelsey Luther
Art direction by Rita Marshall
Printed in China

Photographs by Alamy (Petr Bonek, Boaz Rottem), Dreamstime (Ken Backer, Fat'fa'tin, Kjeld Friis, Hel080808, Gunter Hofer, Kristy Johnson, Garcia Juan, Lisa Mckown, Mdvejby, Pgaborphotos, Unholyvault, Jiri Vaclavek), Getty Images (Apic, Kevin Cruff), National Geographic Creative (O. LOUIS MAZZATENTA), Shutterstock (Kanuman, underworld)

Library of Congress Cataloging-in-Publication Data
Names: Bodden, Valerie, author.
Tombs / Valerie Bodden.
Series: Creep out.
Includes bibliographical references and index.
Summary: Feel goosebumps begin to form as this title explores tombs around the world, surveying common tomb features and creepy stories about these places.

Identifiers: LCCN 2016033591 / ISBN 978-1-60818-810-9 (hardcover) / ISBN 978-1-56660-858-9 (eBook)
Subjects: LCSH: 1. Tombs—Psychological aspects—Juvenile literature. 2. Haunted places—Juvenile literature. 3. Parapsychology—Juvenile literature.
Classification: LCC BF1461.B635 2017 / DDC 133.1/22—dc23

CCSS: RI.1.1, 2, 3, 4, 5, 6, 10; RI.2.1, 2, 3, 4, 5, 6, 7, 10; RI.3.1, 2, 3, 4, 5, 10; RF.1.1, 3, 4; RF.2.3, 4; RF.3.3, 4

First Edition HC 9 8 7 6 5 4 3 2 1

Table *of* Contents

INTRODUCTION 4

RESTING PLACES 7

WHAT MAKES TOMBS CREEPY? 10

FAMOUS TOMBS 13

CREEP OUT! 19

DIAGRAM OF A TOMB 20

GLOSSARY 22

READ MORE 23

WEBSITES 23

INDEX 24

Introduction

You strain your ears but hear only silence. Strange writing covers stone walls. Damp, musty air clings to your skin. You shiver. You are in a tomb.

THIS PASSAGE TOMB IN IRELAND IS BENEATH A LARGE MOUND OF EARTH AND ROCK.

Resting Places

TOMBS are chambers, or rooms, for dead bodies. Many tombs are underground. Others are built into hills or caves. Some are marked by huge pyramids.

THE CRYPT AT THE ANCIENT CITY OF PETRA WAS BUILT ABOUT 2,000 YEARS AGO.

TREASURES FROM TOMBS MAY END UP IN MUSEUMS OR STORAGE PLACES FOR SAFEKEEPING.

PEOPLE have built tombs for thousands of years. The world's biggest tombs were built for kings. The kings were buried with gold, jewelry, and weapons. Sometimes they were buried with food and servants, too. People thought the rulers needed these things in the afterlife.

What Makes Tombs Creepy?

TOMBS creep some people out. Most tombs are dark. They might have secret rooms. Some have booby traps. In many tombs, sarcophagi (*sar-KOFF-uh-guy*) hold mummies. Other tombs contain bones.

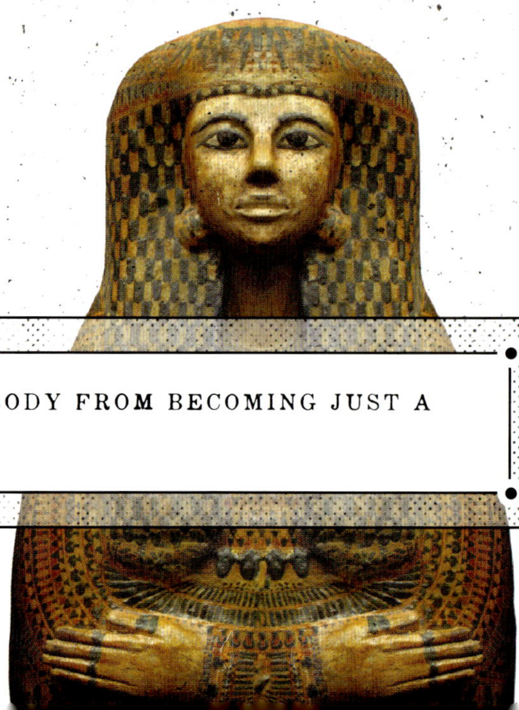

A SARCOPHAGUS PROTECTS A BODY FROM BECOMING JUST A PILE OF BONES.

Famous Tombs

The Valley of the Kings is in Egypt. It holds the tombs of many Egyptian kings. Robbers stole most things from the tombs. But King Tut's tomb was found in 1922. The king's mummy was still in the tomb. Some people say King Tut's tomb is cursed.

ENGLISH ARCHAEOLOGIST HOWARD CARTER WAS ONE OF THE DISCOVERERS OF KING TUT'S TOMB.

CHINA'S first emperor was named Qin Shi Huangdi. He built a huge tomb for himself. The tomb holds more than 8,000 clay soldiers. The emperor's burial chamber has not been dug out. But records say it is booby-trapped.

THE SIZES OF THE CLAY STATUES ARE DIFFERENT, DEPENDING ON THE RANK OF THE SOLDIER.

EURAC

THE Palermo monastery is in Italy. It holds many mummies. They were dressed in clothes. Then they were hung on the walls. Their loved ones came to visit.

THE FIRST MONK BURIED IN THE CATACOMBS (UNDERGROUND CEMETERY) OF PALERMO WAS DISPLAYED IN 1599.

Creep Out!

TODAY, people can tour many tombs. Are you brave enough to enter? Or will you get creeped out?

ANCIENT WARRIORS WERE OFTEN BURIED WITH THEIR WEAPONS AND SHIELDS.

Diagram *of a* Tomb

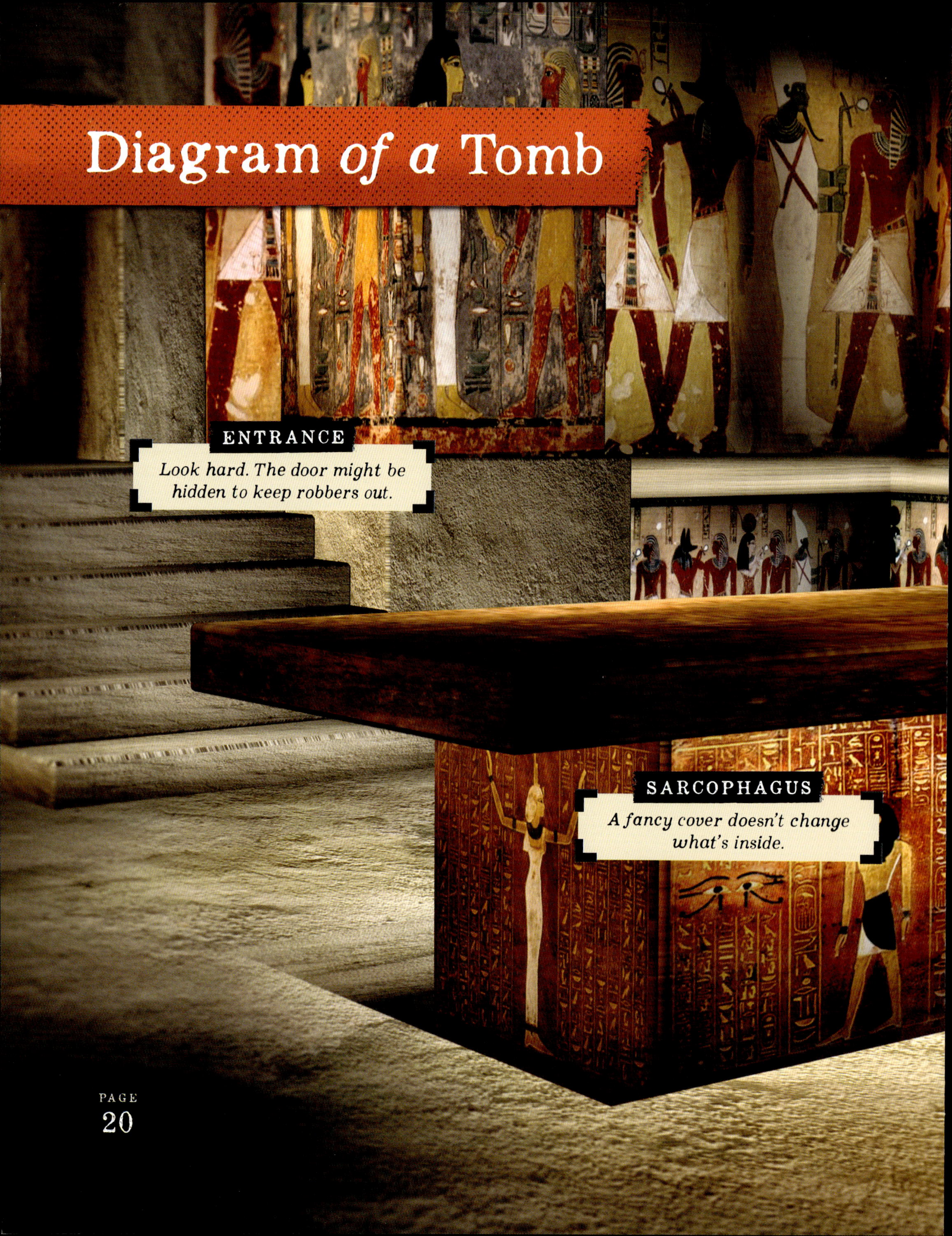

MUMMY

Look for his organs *in jars nearby.*

SKELETONS

These might be from servants buried with their king.

TREASURE

Touch it if you dare. Do you believe in the mummy's curse?

Glossary

AFTERLIFE—a life that some people believe starts after a person dies

BOOBY TRAPS—hidden weapons set to go off when someone moves or touches an object

CURSED—something believed to have an evil spell on it

EMPEROR—a ruler of an empire, or large area of land and peoples

MONASTERY—a place where religious men known as monks live

ORGANS—body parts, such as the kidneys, that do a special job

SARCOPHAGI—stone boxes to hold dead bodies; one box is called a sarcophagus

Read More

Owings, Lisa. *The Mummy's Curse.* Minneapolis: Bellwether Media, 2015.

Riggs, Kate. *Egyptian Pyramids.* Mankato, Minn.: Creative Education, 2009.

Websites

Discovery Kids: Mummy Maker

http://discoverykids.com/games/mummy-maker/

Play a game to make your own mummy.

National Geographic: Unraveling the Mysteries of King Tutankhamun

http://ngm.nationalgeographic.com/static-legacy/ngm/tut/mysteries/

Check out videos of King Tut's tomb, and learn more about mummies.

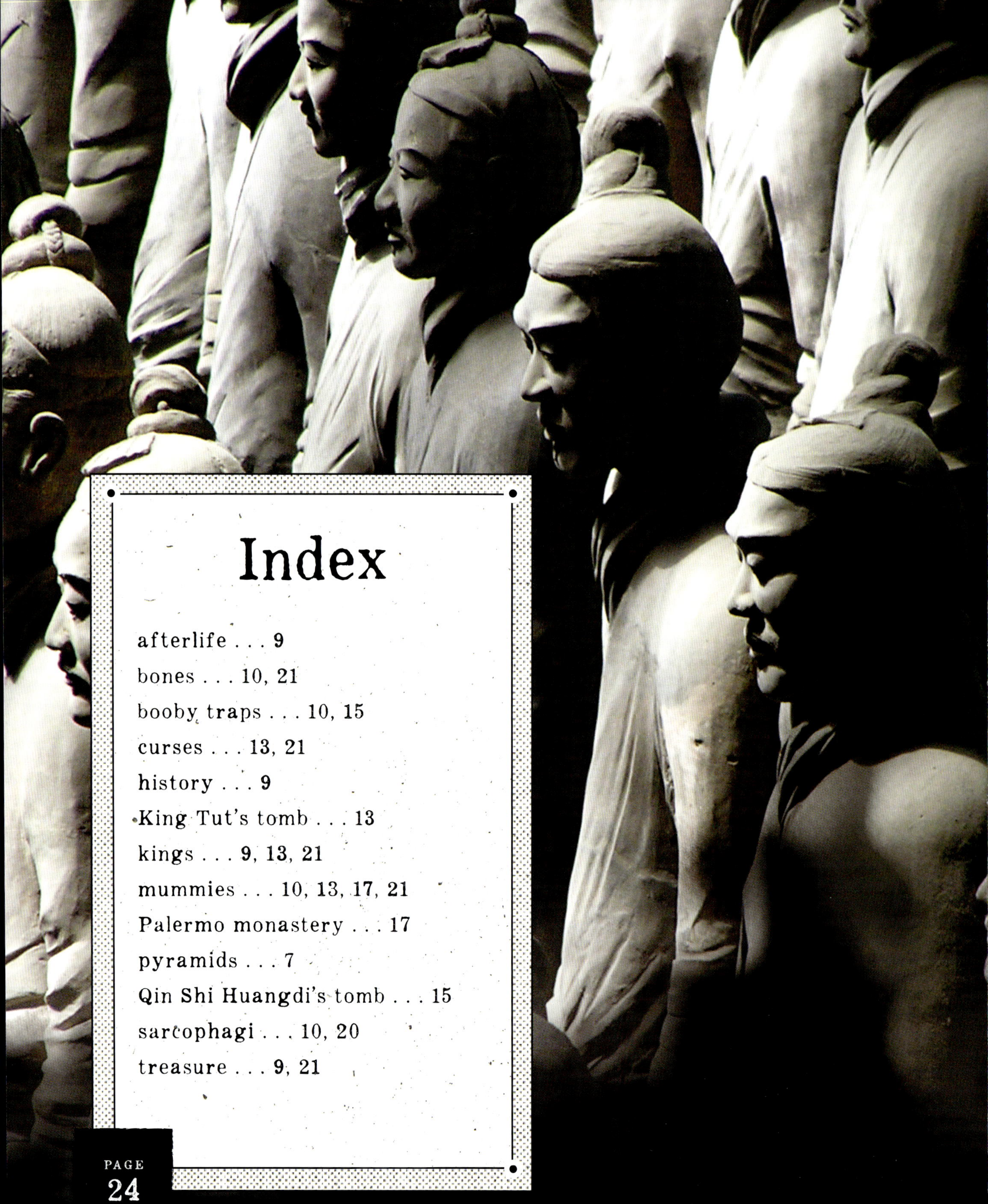

Index

afterlife . . . 9

bones . . . 10, 21

booby traps . . . 10, 15

curses . . . 13, 21

history . . . 9

King Tut's tomb . . . 13

kings . . . 9, 13, 21

mummies . . . 10, 13, 17, 21

Palermo monastery . . . 17

pyramids . . . 7

Qin Shi Huangdi's tomb . . . 15

sarcophagi . . . 10, 20

treasure . . . 9, 21